4 741911 000

PUZZLE JOURNEYS

Rebecca Heddle and Lesley Sims

Illustrated by Sue Stitt and Annabel Spenceley

Cover illustration by Sue Stitt

Space consultant: Martin Lunn
History consultant: Anne Millard BA, PhD

Contents

Designed by Lucy Parris, Kim Blundell
and Amanda Barlow
Edited by Jenny Tyler
Series Editor: Gaby Waters

PUZZLE JOURNEY AROUND THE WORLD

Here are Eli, Su and Em. They are out shopping with Aunt Rose. But she keeps stopping to chat and they're feeling fed-up. Little do they know that an exciting adventure is about to happen.

Eli

Su

Em

The adventure will take them on an amazing journey all around the world. They'll face lots of challenging puzzles on the way. See if you can solve them too. There are answers at the end of the story if you get stuck.

The junk shop

"Meet you back here in twenty minutes!" Aunt Rose had said and disappeared.

So Em, Su and Eli were left in the hot, stuffy mall, waiting for her.

"This is boring," said Em. "Let's go for a walk."

They wandered outside. Before long, they were in a part of town they hadn't visited before.

There were other stores to look at, but it still wasn't much fun. Then Eli found one that looked different.

"Let's go in here," he called to the other two, as he opened the door. A bell jangled noisily.

Inside, they found the oddest collection of things. Eli picked up a globe half-heartedly. All at once, he had a strange feeling that he had to buy it.

"You really want that old thing?" the lady asked him. Eli nodded. "There's a bag to go with it somewhere," she said, describing it.

"They have to be sold together. Don't ask me why!" She looked around, but she couldn't find it.

Can you find the bag?

3

Egbert the explorer?

"I'm afraid the globe and bag are very battered," the lady told Eli. "They belonged to my great-grandfather Egbert." She pointed to a painting.

"That's him. He always wanted to be an explorer. Instead, he had to work in a bank." She smiled. "So he spent all his time daydreaming."

"He pretended he'd been all over the world. He lived in a world of his own more like. Well, enjoy your geography lessons," she laughed, as Eli paid her.

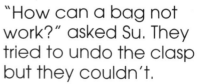

This bag will work anywhere in the world!

With Eli hugging the globe, they left the shop. Su and Em swung the bag between them.

Suddenly, Em stopped. "Hey, there's a label tied to the handle," she said. She read it out.

"How can a bag not work?" asked Su. They tried to undo the clasp but they couldn't.

"We don't need the bag," said Eli. But Em wouldn't give up. She pulled at the clasp so hard, she fell over.

Em fell on Su who fell on Eli. The globe crashed to the ground and broke in two. "Can we glue it?" said Em.

She held the halves together. As if by magic, the globe was whole again. They were amazed.

The key inside this cheer-up box. But you each country I visited,

Happy
Egbert

This is a magical world with it and you you everywhere I went. are shown in my portrait. globe will take you to the

Dear Fellow Explorer,

globe opens my special will only reach it if you visit and collect all of my things.

exploring!
Boff

globe. I went all over the can too. The globe will take Look out for the things that When you find one, the next place.

"Look!" said Su. "Something's fallen out of the globe."

It was a piece of paper as thin as a butterfly's wing. As Su unfolded it, the paper fell apart and a key fell out.

Whatever could it open? Su put the letter together, to see if it told her.

Can you help her piece together the letter? What does it say?

5

On safari

"Exploring?" said Eli. He began to feel excited. "A special box? And all we have to do is find Egbert's things?" Em and Su's eyes lit up for a second.

"But the lady said he only pretended to explore," Su said. Eli looked at the globe again. Under his fingers, it was beginning to spin.

It spun faster and faster. The whole world became a whirling merry-go-round. Suddenly it stopped. Em, Su and Eli swayed where they stood, feeling dizzy.

They could hardly believe their eyes. The shop had vanished. "Isn't it hot," said Em. "What's happened?"

"Wow," said Su. "Maybe the globe *is* magic."

"A lion?" cried Eli. "RUN!"

They scrambled up a tree for safety. Eli gazed at all the animals around them. "We're in Africa," he said.

The lion ambled away. Eli started to climb down. He wanted a closer look at the zebras. But a twig caught his T-shirt. He wriggled, almost knocking a nest off its branch.

Then he saw something inside the nest. He recognized it at once from the painting of Egbert in the junk shop.

What has Eli spotted?

On top of the world

This looks like my poster of the Himalayas!

Eli grasped the telescope. None of them saw the globe begin to turn. It whirled them away.

They landed on a high mountain peak. "I wanted to explore Africa," Em moaned. "Where are we?"

Eli felt peculiar. He didn't like being so high. The globe fell from his hands. Su dived after it.

Too late. The three of them watched in horror as it bounced down a ravine.

As it fell, the globe spun. They spun too, landing on a path in front of a hut.

The globe was a long way down. It would be tricky, but they had to rescue it.

"Look what I've found," said Su. She held up a rope and two sturdy sticks. "We can use these to climb down, like hikers."

"But there are three of us," said Em. "We'll need another stick."

"I can see one," called Eli.

Leaning against some rocks, was a walking stick carved with the familiar letters EB. Eli gripped it and held on tight.

Su took the telescope. "The globe's trapped near a bridge. Hold the rope and follow me."

Can you find a safe way down?

Sun and sand

As Eli freed the globe, it spun. The mountains melted away and they fell through space.

They landed, *bump!* on scorching sand. The air was hot and dry. "We must be in a desert," said Su.

The bag burst open as it hit the sand. Three scarves trailed out. Em tugged one. "Let's put them on."

As they wound the scarves around them, a line of people and camels appeared. Quickly, they hid behind a bush.

A man in a white scarf put up his hand. The camels stopped. "This is good," the man said. "We shall make camp here."

"We've just done this at school," Eli murmured, looking at the man. "These people are nomads. They travel all over the Sahara."

A boy about Eli's age, carried a baby goat over to their bush. "Who are you?" he asked in surprise. "Were you separated from your tribe?"

Before they could answer, a man shouted, "Akhaya!" The boy turned. "It's my job to fetch the water," he told them. Where from? Em wondered.

The boy rode a camel with a rope tied to its saddle. As he rode away, a bag of water rose out of the ground. It was a well in the middle of the desert.

Su licked her dry lips. "I've never felt so thirsty in my life," she whispered. A smell of cooking filled the air. Eli's tummy rumbled.

The boy from the camel spoke to the man in the white scarf. Then he waved the three over. "Come, my father says eat with us."

As they walked to the tents, Eli grabbed Su's arm in excitement. "I can see something of Egbert's," he said.

Can you?

11

A wide, dark river

Eli was given the spoon. Now they had three things in the bag. Where would the globe go next?

It grew hot and damp. Branches above them hid the sky. The air was full of buzzing and humming.

They were on a river bank. Eli nearly fell in. "Look out, there might be crocodiles," said Su.

A large can poked out of the bag. Su shook it and sprayed it all over them.

"Yeuch! That's disgusting," Eli spluttered. "It smells like rotting hamburgers."

Em pointed to a huge, spotty flower. "The smell's coming from that."

"Squark!" said a voice and they jumped. A suspicious parrot had fixed two beady eyes on them.

Su saw a gliding tree frog. "They really glide," she said. "And suckers on their toes stick to the trees."

"Hey," said Em, waving the telescope at a tree. "I can see Egbert's helmet. It's been used as a nest."

12

Su was the best climber so she went to get it. Vines hung down around her. She used them to climb up the trunk.

Em watched Su go higher. Then, to her amazement, she saw a twig begin to crawl. It was a stick insect.

Em and Eli looked more closely. Lots of creatures were cleverly disguised, to merge into the jungle around them.

I've just seen a snake and a moth.

I can see a chameleon and a turtle.

"Got it," Su called, clutching the helmet. All of a sudden, she looked terrified. "This tree is dangerous. Come on globe. Spin NOW!"

Can you spot the creatures they saw? Do you know what scared Su?

Monkey mischief

"That was a narrow escape," said Em. "Where are we now?" They stood in a hot, noisy, busy street.

Su smiled. "I know," she said. "My Gran's told me so much about it – India."

A boy rushed past them, carrying a carpet. "It's the same as Egbert's scarf in the picture," cried Em. "Let's follow him."

The boy paused to talk to the driver of a little yellow cab. Then he vanished down a side street. "We'll never find him now," Su panted.

But the driver heard her. "The boy is my cousin," he told them. "He works at the Carpet Emporium, most beautiful of all carpet makers. Would you like a lift?"

The second they climbed aboard, they were off. The driver sped along, not stopping for anyone. It was a very bumpy ride.

At last, he stopped outside a low, white house. A man with a big smile welcomed them. "Hello! You wish to buy a carpet, no?"

"Er, no," said Su. She pointed to a half-made carpet. "We're looking for a scarf with that pattern. It's quite old."

"This dirty old rag?" said the man, holding out a scarf. "No, we'll make you a fine, new one."

"We *really* like that one," said Su. The man was baffled. He shrugged and gave it to them.

Outside, disaster struck. A monkey snatched the scarf. "Hey, we need that," Eli yelled, giving chase.

The monkey scampered down the street. Soon he was lost in the turmoil of people and animals.

"I can't see him anywhere," Eli said sadly. Su couldn't see him either. Just then, Em spotted him.

Where is the monkey?

The island in the lake

Em threw some nuts to the monkey. Su took the scarf. The globe turned . . .

. . . and they were on an island. The sun shone brightly but it felt very cold.

Then the bag sprang open. Inside were pullovers and woolly hats with ear flaps.

They were pulling the clothes on when a boy walked up to them.

"Hello," said the boy. "Did you come over with the floating market?"

Eli looked blank. Where were they? They went from place to place so quickly.

A girl tugged the boy's sleeve. "Sergio, we must go or we'll miss the race. They've already started building the boats."

"OK Luisa," the boy smiled. "Today's the Lake Titicaca boat race," he explained. "Our father builds the best reed boats in all Bolivia!"

On the shore, people were twisting thick bundles of reeds. Eli, Em and Su watched astounded, as the boats took shape.

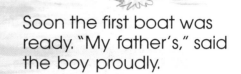

Soon the first boat was ready. "My father's," said the boy proudly.

But as his father was launching the boat, he tripped and hurt his arm.

Now he couldn't row. The boy's face fell. His father had worked so quickly. But he had lost before the race had even started.

"I'll row," Em cried. She seized the oar and was off. Em rowed frantically. A second boat was right on her tail.

Em rowed faster still. She shot past the finish. She'd won. The boy's father was thrilled. "The prize is yours," he said. "You earned it."

As Em took her prize, the globe began to spin. "Why did you do it?" Eli asked her.

Do you know why?

Children's Day

The globe whizzed around. Towering skyscrapers loomed over them. Then POP!

They were in a crowded park. As she landed, Em burst a boy's balloon. He cried out in surprise.

"Sorry," said Em. "I didn't see you. Where are we?"

The boy was bewildered. "In Japan, of course," he said. He bowed. "My name is Takashi. Who are you?" Su told him. She wondered if she should bow too.

"Where did you come from?" Takashi asked. Eli looked at the others and then the globe. Should he explain about Egbert? Su and Em nodded. The whole story came out.

"I know of Explorer Boff," said Takashi. The others were startled. How could he know about Egbert?

"If you come to tea to celebrate Children's Day, my father can tell you all about him," Takashi said.

A giant cloth fish hung outside his house. Puffed up with wind, it looked as if it was swimming in the air.

Inside, they sat around a low table. Noodles sizzled and spat on a hot plate. But Eli couldn't use his chopsticks. "It takes practice," said Takashi.

"Mr. Boff met my grandfather," Takashi's father told them. "Mr. Boff gave him a box as a gift. My grandfather planted a tree in it. Please take it."

What could they give him? Su thought back. When they'd put on the pullovers, she'd seen the very thing.

Did you spot it too?

A red rock and a thirsty frog

As Takashi untied the ribbon on the box, the globe whisked them away. They were somewhere very hot with strange trees.

A kangaroo bounded past. Then they saw two koalas in a tree. There was no mistaking where they were now – Australia.

Three hats flew out of the bag. Em caught one. At the same time, Su spotted a boomerang behind a bush.

I bet it's the biggest rock in the world!

But as she went to pick it up, the globe spun. "Hey, stop! We've only just arrived," cried Eli. His voice was drowned out by a loud booming.

"Wanna go inside the rock?" asked a man in red shorts. Eli, Em and Su followed a family of tourists into the cave.

Can you guess how the rock came to be here? Once upon a time, it was a frog! The biggest frog in the world. And this desert was its ocean.

All day long, the frog caught flies and swam. At night he slept on a lily pad. Until, one day, he woke up feeling very thirsty.

He drank and drank until he had emptied the ocean. There wasn't a drop of water left. And that's why there's only sand here today.

The man began to tell them a story in a sing-song voice. When the story ended, the tourists trailed out of the cave.

But Em had spotted something in a gap between the rocks. She went closer to investigate. A book was poking out.

Its pages crackled as Em picked it up. The book looked old and dirty and there was a strange label on the front cover.

At first, the label didn't make sense. Then Em realized it was in code. As she read it, the globe began to spin.

What does the label say?

YM YRAID
YB
TREBGE
FFOB

Finding the way

Trees whirled around them. They were back in a forest. But it wasn't as damp as the Amazon.

Eli was holding the bag. All of a sudden, it sprang open. A note from Egbert flew out. It said he had left his compass behind in a house in the forest, and told them how to find it.

Can you find the house where Egbert left his compass?

Malaysia, April 2nd: Left my compass behind when I had lunch with some villagers. To reach their house, take the right-hand fork outside the Headman's house, (the only green one in the village), then the second path on the left. There are two tall palm trees on the right, just after a bridge. At the very end of that path turn right. Their house is the blue hut opposite you. It stands beside a large tree close to the river.

Windmills and tulips

The compass was hanging from a tree outside the house. The globe turned and they were off again.

"Wow," cried Su. They had landed on bikes, which somehow seemed to know where to go.

Alongside them, windmills were pumping water. "This is Holland," said Em. "My cousin came here."

One of the windmills had a balcony. People were looking out. "Maybe we can climb up too," Su said.

There were lots of tourists. Leaving their bikes at the door, they went in. Ladders led up to different platforms. One by one, they panted to the top.

Eli took out Egbert's telescope. "There aren't any hills," he said in surprise. At that moment, without warning, a breeze lifted one of the windmill's arms.

The bag was hooked up by a handle. It swung into the air and hovered over them, almost out of reach. Su leapt to the rescue and only just caught it.

Feeling very relieved, they went back inside. A man was telling the visitors all about windmills.

"Millers sent each other messages by putting a windmill's arms in a certain position. They tied the sails on in different ways too."

Em had found a leaflet which showed some of the messages. She read it out to the others.

> Some mills are used to grind corn. This one used to pump water. Now it's just for tourists!

VERTICAL SHAFT

CROWN WHEEL

PIT WHEEL

TAKE A PAIR HOME!

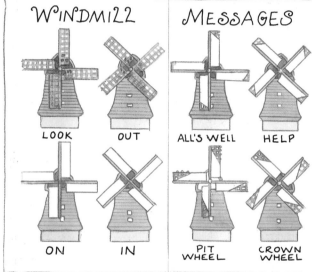

WINDMILL

LOOK

OUT

ON

IN

MESSAGES

ALL'S WELL

HELP

PIT WHEEL

CROWN WHEEL

Eli looked out of a window and saw a line of mills in the distance. "Hey," he said. "I think they have a message for us."

What does the message say?

Snowballs and surprises

There on the wheel were Egbert's clogs. Su picked them up. They were off.

But the globe stopped and they were left adrift. "It's stuck," Eli cried in a panic.

A chill wind blew around them. "Are there coats in the bag?" Su shivered.

Delving down, they found padded clothes, goggles and boots. When they were well wrapped up, the globe spun once more.

They landed somewhere cold and glistening white. Gulls screeched and slid on icebergs. Seals honked and flapped their flippers.

"This must be the North Pole," cried Em. "It's completely made of ice floating on the sea. There's no land at all."

Su wondered where the penguins were. "That's the South Pole," said Eli.

26

Em saw a hole in the ice and three rods. "Look, we can fish through the ice."

"I've got a bite," cried Su. But she didn't have a fish on the end of her line.

Just then, they heard loud creaking and cracking noises.

Eli smiled. "I remember reading about this," he said. "The ice makes those noises as it moves."

"But what's the hump over there?" Su asked. "A polar bear?" They crept up on it silently. It didn't move.

"It's an igloo," said Em, "A shelter made of snow. They're used by people on hunting trips."

"This is great," said Eli. "The globe isn't in such a hurry for once."

"Maybe it's frozen," said Su.

Why do you think the globe hasn't spun yet?

27

Journey's end

Em picked up Egbert's sock and the globe spun faster than ever. When it stopped, they were on the beach of a tropical island. A cross had been drawn in the sand.

"The cheer-up box!" cried Eli. It had been such an exciting day, they'd almost forgotten the key in the globe. Beside the sandy cross were three spades. Eli, Em and Su began to dig.

At long last, Em's spade hit something hard. She threw down the spade. Then she used her hands to scrape the sand away.

Carefully, Em lifted a small, wooden box out of the hole. Su fished for the key in her pocket. She put it in the lock and turned . . .

. . . click! The box flew open. Inside was a scrap of paper. "Still feeling fed-up?" it read. Eli laughed. "No," he said.

In a blink of an eye they were back home.

"Let's take Egbert's things to the lady in the shop," said Em. "We can tell her that he *was* an explorer after all."

Su looked inside the bag. "They're not here," she cried. Eli took the bag and turned it upside down. Souvenirs they had been given or found along the way fell out. But all of Egbert's things had gone.

"Maybe it's so someone else can find them," said Eli. "Come on, let's take back the globe and bag."

Before they do, look back. Can you spot where each souvenir came from?

Around the world

Back at the mall, they were amazed. Barely ten minutes had passed. Moments later, Aunt Rose arrived, very surprised at their sudden interest in geography.

She bought them a World Encyclopedia, for waiting so patiently. They found out lots more about the places they'd seen. Here is a page from their scrapbook.

The tree we climbed in Africa is called a Baobab. It takes up lots of water when it rains and stores it in its trunk. That's why it always looks so fat.

Water lilies on the Amazon river can grow to over 1m (1.094 yds) in diameter. The smelly plant is called a rafflesia.

In India, cows are sacred. They wander all over the street and the traffic has to go around them.

Ayers Rock in Australia belongs to the Aborigines, the first people to live in Australia. They call it Uluru. It is 600 million years old.

The fox at the North Pole was an Arctic fox. It's like European ones, but its coat is white. This makes it harder to see in the snow.

Bolivia is in South America. The lake we saw is the highest in the world that's big enough to sail on.

The fish hanging outside Takashi's house was a carp. In Japan, it means strength and determination.

さかな

Holland is part of the Netherlands. Years ago, people there wore wooden shoes called clogs. Now they are mostly made for visitors.

Answers

pages 2-3
The junk shop

The bag is by Eli's foot. It has been circled in this picture.

pages 4-5
Egbert the explorer?

When the letter is put together, it says:

Dear Fellow Explorer,

This is a magical globe. I went all over the world with it and you can too. The globe will take you everywhere I went. Look out for the things that are shown in my portrait. When you find one, the globe will take you to the next place.

The key inside this globe opens my special cheer-up box. But you will only reach it if you visit each country I visited, and collect all of my things.

Happy exploring!
Egbert Boff

pages 6-7
On safari

Eli has spotted Egbert's telescope. Here you can see it in the nest.

pages 8-9
On top of the world

The safe way to the globe is shown in red.

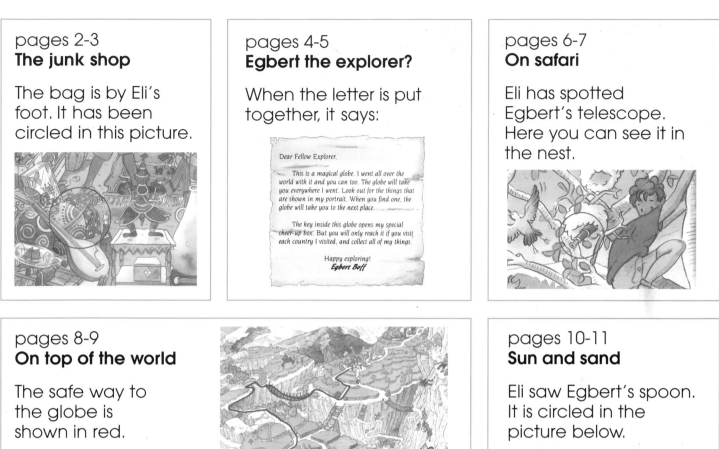

pages 10-11
Sun and sand

Eli saw Egbert's spoon. It is circled in the picture below.

pages 12-13
A wide, dark river

Su saw a jaguar in the tree. It is circled here, with the other creatures Em and Eli spotted.

snake   moth

jaguar

chameleon

turtle

pages 14-15
Monkey mischief

The monkey has climbed up a lamppost. You can see it circled below.

pages 16-17
The island in the lake

Em rowed because she had seen the prize – Egbert's hunting knife. It is circled below.

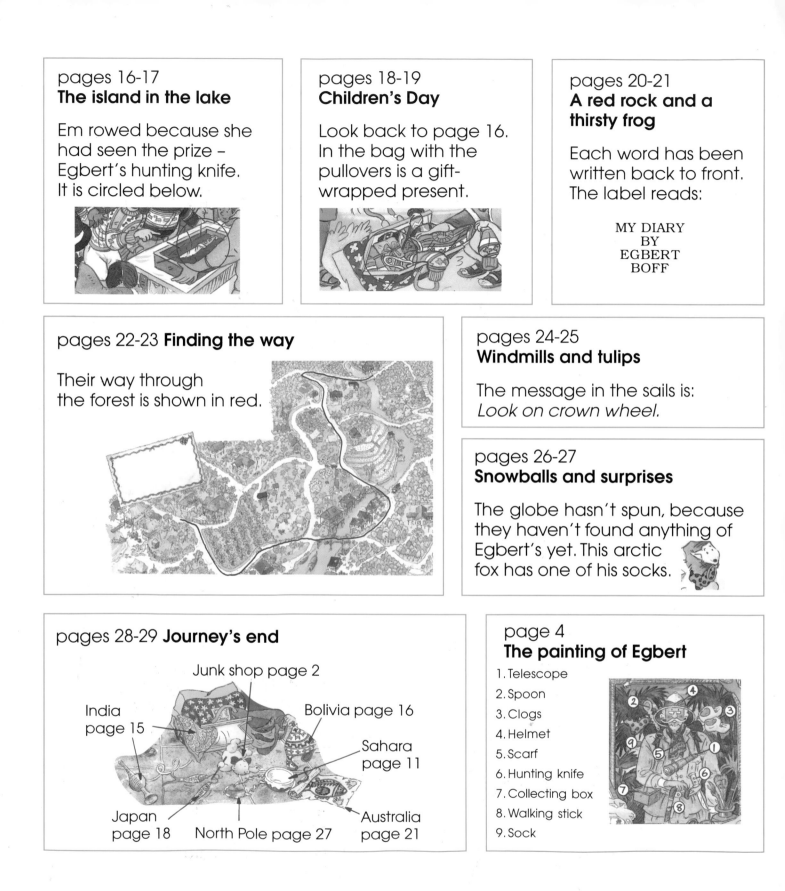

pages 18-19
Children's Day

Look back to page 16. In the bag with the pullovers is a gift-wrapped present.

pages 20-21
A red rock and a thirsty frog

Each word has been written back to front. The label reads:

MY DIARY
BY
EGBERT
BOFF

pages 22-23 **Finding the way**

Their way through the forest is shown in red.

pages 24-25
Windmills and tulips

The message in the sails is: *Look on crown wheel.*

pages 26-27
Snowballs and surprises

The globe hasn't spun, because they haven't found anything of Egbert's yet. This arctic fox has one of his socks.

pages 28-29 **Journey's end**

Junk shop page 2

India page 15

Bolivia page 16

Sahara page 11

Japan page 18

North Pole page 27

Australia page 21

page 4
The painting of Egbert

1. Telescope
2. Spoon
3. Clogs
4. Helmet
5. Scarf
6. Hunting knife
7. Collecting box
8. Walking stick
9. Sock

PUZZLE JOURNEY INTO SPACE

This ticket entitles the holder to an exciting adventure in Space!

SPACE IS FULL OF SURPRISES

SPACE EXPERIENCE

SO PREPARE TO BE AMAZED

Welcome to
The Space Experience -
so real you'll think you're there!

Joe

Nat

This story is all about an incredible journey into space. It begins with Nat and Joe and their school trip to a museum, but it turns into a thrilling adventure. Along the way Nat and Joe have different puzzles to solve. See if you can solve them too. There are answers at the end of the story if you are stuck.

A new spaceship

Nat and Joe were on a school trip to the Space Experience, the biggest space museum in the world.

As they waited to go in, Nat grew more and more excited. "I want to be an astronaut," she said.

Joe grunted. He wasn't interested in space and he didn't like museums. "I'd rather be playing football," he muttered.

Ryan Rocket

Alien ship?

Landed on Earth 1995

When they got inside at last, they saw a spacesuit and shiny models of rockets and satellites on display.

There were huge pictures of planets and far-off galaxies covering the walls. But Joe was bored.

Models and pictures weren't much fun. Then he felt Nat tugging the back of his t-shirt.

"Follow me!" she said. "I've found something much more exciting."

She dragged Joe along a corridor lined with photographs and posters.

"This doesn't look any more interesting to me," he grumbled.

It's just a big plane!

But the corridor led into an enormous hall which was almost filled by a plane.

"Look!" said Nat. "It's a model of the very latest space shuttle!"

She dashed inside. "What are you doing?" said Joe and followed her.

What's happening?

Nat sat down in front of a screen and eagerly hit a few buttons. Suddenly the doors slid shut.

In a panic Joe tried to open them. Nat didn't even notice. She was too busy playing astronauts.

"Three... two... one... Lift off!" said Nat as a joke. But the cockpit filled with a loud roaring noise.

Into space

Joe quickly sat down beside Nat and they stared out of the window. They could see the whole Earth in it and it was growing smaller and smaller.

"This model spaceship is great!" said Joe. "It really feels as if we've taken off."

Look at the Earth!

IT'S ONLY A TOOL LEFT BEHIND BY SOME CARELESS ASTRONAUT. THERE ARE MORE THAN 7,000 PIECES OF JUNK UP HERE.

Nat was amazed too. But before she could reply, an object drifted across a screen in front of them.

"What's that?" asked Nat. As she spoke a message appeared on the screen with the answer.

"Do you think the ship can hear us?" she asked Joe in surprise. Joe wasn't listening. He was staring at the screen again.

Now it showed the moon, growing bigger and bigger. Then it appeared in the window, dusty grey and covered with craters.

Seconds later, they felt a gentle thud. The noise from the engines stopped.

"It's incredible!" cried Joe. "It's just as if we've landed on the moon."

36

"Let's see what it's like outside," said Nat. "We'll need spacesuits." She jumped up and began searching through all the drawers in the cabin.

Joe was doubtful. "We're still in the museum," he said. "Outside it's just that big hall."

But Nat had found two large white suits and some jumbo-sized gloves.

TOOLS PENS BOOKS PENC
FOOD PERS. SEEDS TRAYS
CHEM GLASS MED KIT PIPES
T. TU
SCISSORS BEAK
KNIVES GLOVES
HELM

"I wonder what it's like to walk on the moon," she said, struggling into the strange space underwear.

"We'll never know," said Joe's muffled voice, from under his bulky jacket. Nat ignored him.

"Now where are the helmets?" she wondered.

Do you know?

37

Walking on the moon

Just wearing the suits made them feel excited as they left the cabin. It seemed to take ages for the outer door to open. When it finally slid back they stared out in astonishment, hardly believing their eyes.

"Wow! It really looks like the moon!" said Nat, as she climbed down the ladder.

"It's weird, I feel so light!" said Joe delightedly, as he jumped off the bottom rung.

Nat followed more slowly. The big suit and boots were hard to move in, although they weren't heavy. Joe was jumping around as if his boots had springs on.

On the last rung Nat paused. Here goes! she thought and stepped off the ladder.

Joe grinned and said something but Nat couldn't hear a word he was saying.

Why was he mouthing words at her? Nat wondered. He looked like an excited goldfish.

Then she remembered. In space, astronauts used radios in their suits to talk to each other.

Joe jogged up to a large boulder and kicked it. "It's a goal!" he cried as the rock bounced away.

"These rocks are as light as beach balls," Joe said, lifting one above his head. "Hey Nat, catch!"

Nat looked up to see a huge rock flying straight at her. She hit it back gently and it soared past Joe.

It flew over his head and landed near a flag of stars and stripes.

"This was left by the first men on the moon," said Nat. "Their footprints are still here! There's no wind or rain to wash them away."

She looked at the ground. "That's odd!" she said.

What has Nat noticed?

39

Men on the moon?

Joe and Nat were carried inside and left in front of a large screen. They were terrified. What was going on?

Suddenly a picture appeared. To their surprise it showed a man sitting behind a large control panel, in a room full of machines.

317 *
to call
robots to
base

"Have you stolen a spaceship?" asked the man on the screen. "Oh dear." He made the two words sound like a threat.

He scowled at Nat and Joe, as if he could see them through the screen. "Did you think the moon was deserted?" he asked.

Joe was puzzled. He was sure he'd seen the man's face before, but where?

Do you know?

Escape

The man stood up. His image towered over them.

Nat struggled but her robot didn't let go. Then Joe covered the light on his robot and they fell.

As Joe got up, something on the floor caught his eye.

Joe picked it up and raced after Nat to the door. But the robots were close behind.

Nat frantically pushed every button she could see. Finally the buggy started – only just in time.

"Hurry up!" Joe begged looking behind them.

A buggy full of robots was hot on their trail and catching up fast.

Faster!

As they reached the ship, Nat cried out in despair. More robots were already guarding it.

With robots in front and behind, they were trapped. How would they ever escape?

Joe looked at the remote control he'd found. "I think we can give the robots orders with this," he said. "But I don't know which buttons to press."

In a flash, Nat thought of something she'd seen in the angry man's office. "I know the ones we need," she said in relief.

Do you?

Computer speak

Joe and Nat ran into the ship. The doors closed, the engines roared and a strange voice said, "Hi!"

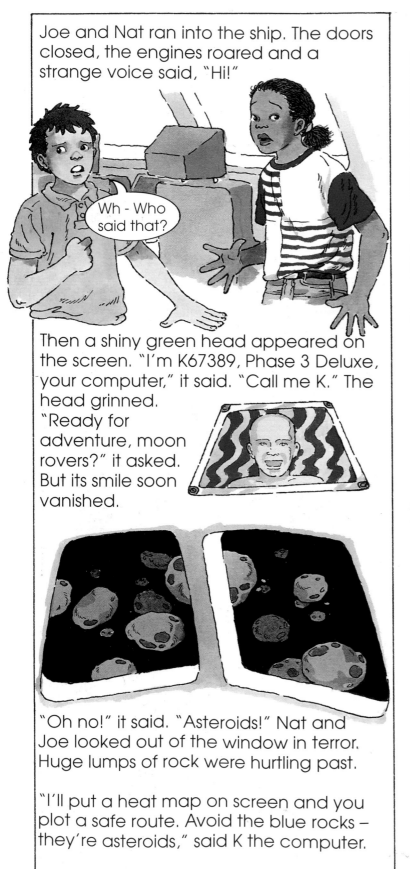

Wh - Who said that?

Then a shiny green head appeared on the screen. "I'm K67389, Phase 3 Deluxe, your computer," it said. "Call me K." The head grinned. "Ready for adventure, moon rovers?" it asked. But its smile soon vanished.

"Oh no!" it said. "Asteroids!" Nat and Joe looked out of the window in terror. Huge lumps of rock were hurtling past.

"I'll put a heat map on screen and you plot a safe route. Avoid the blue rocks – they're asteroids," said K the computer.

Can you find a way through?

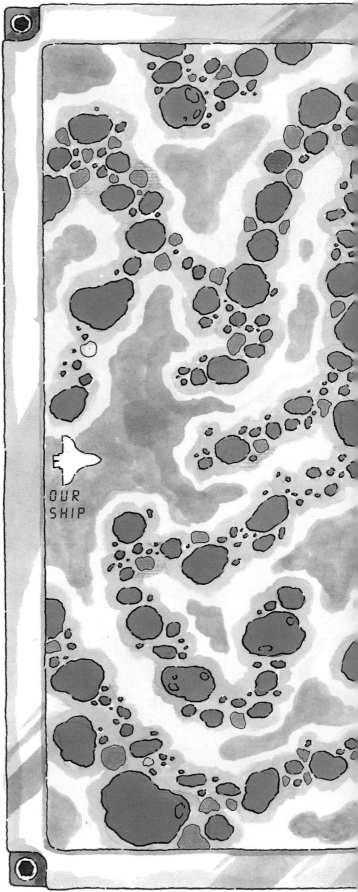

OUR SHIP

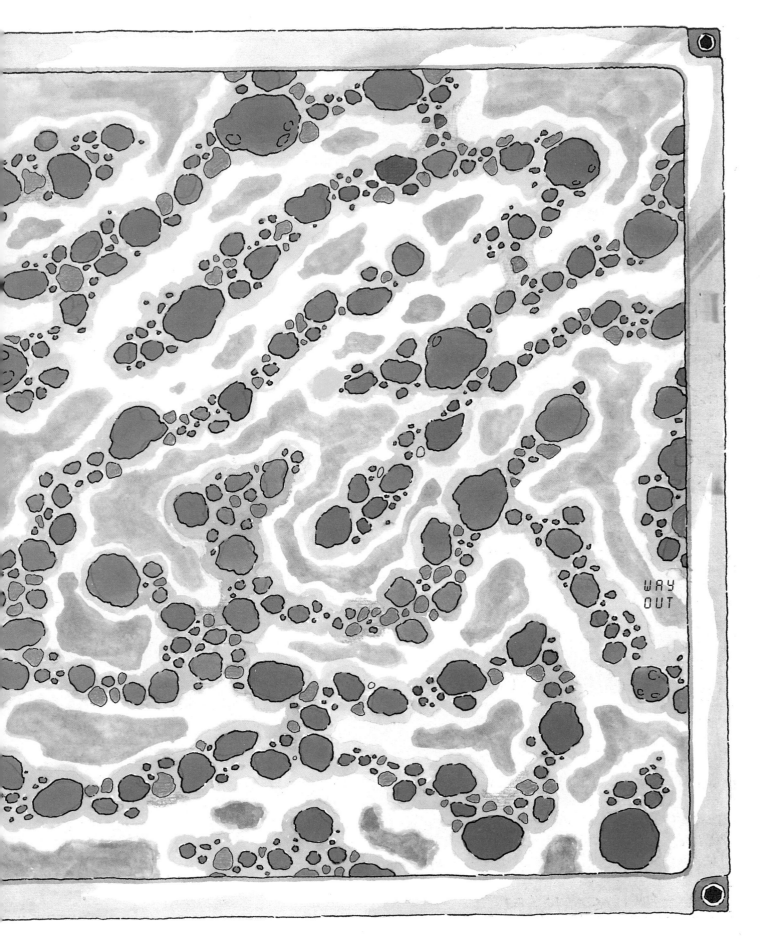

WAY
OUT

45

A gas giant

The ship swung from side to side to avoid the asteroids. Nat and Joe were flung all over the deck.

At last the ship was safely through and flying deeper into space.

A planet loomed up in the window. "That's Jupiter," K told them. "It's big. A thousand times bigger than Earth. But it's mostly made of gas so we can't land on it."

Nat and Joe stared at Jupiter as it came closer. A giant red spot was spinning on the surface.

"That's some storm," said K. "It's been whirling for hundreds of years."

After the bumpy ride through the asteroids, Nat's head was spinning and whirling too.

"I feel sick," she moaned. She staggered back and her elbow accidentally hit a large red button.

Suddenly the ship was thrown on its side, right in the path of an empty spaceship.

"Hang on!" said K, swerving around it. "That was a probe going to Pluto. It won't stop for anything. But we could stop. How about a planet prowl?"

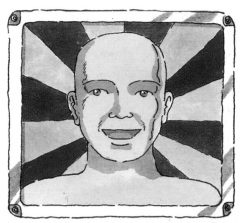

K's head grew big on the screen. "Where shall we land?" he asked. "If I show you a space chart, you can decide."

Is there anywhere we can't land?

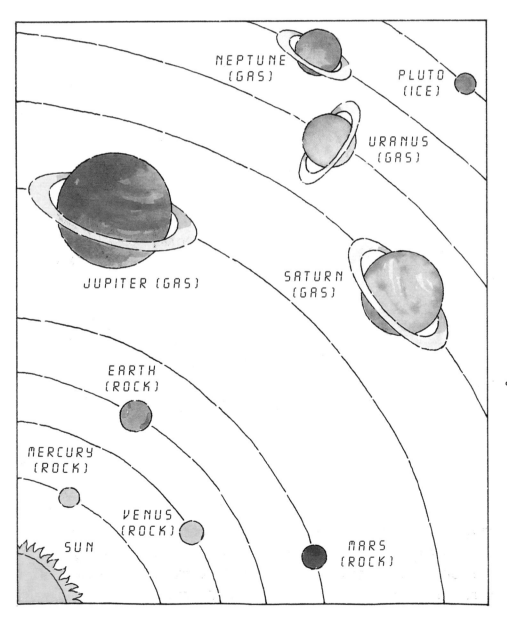

NEPTUNE (GAS)

PLUTO (ICE)

URANUS (GAS)

JUPITER (GAS)

SATURN (GAS)

EARTH (ROCK)

MERCURY (ROCK)

VENUS (ROCK)

SUN

MARS (ROCK)

We can't fly any deeper into space or we won't have fuel to get home. And we can't go closer to the sun than Earth. It's too hot.

Joe and Nat studied the chart. They soon realized that there was only one planet they could land on, apart from Earth.

Which planet is it?

Comet clash

"Mars!" said Nat excitedly, flicking through a book on planets. She read it out to Joe.

It's half the size of Earth. No one has ever walked on it before . . .

Joe didn't hear. He was looking for food. Nat was too excited to eat but space travel had made Joe hungry.

He found several drawers crammed with packets of dried food.

He would have preferred a burger but he heated some anyway.

He ate the food out of the packets. It was very sticky but it tasted really good.

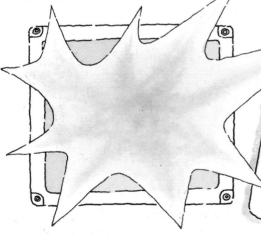

Suddenly, a bright flash filled one screen. "What's that?" said Joe, nearly dropping his tray.

"I think it's a comet going past!" cried Nat. She ran to the window to watch as it shot by.

The comet's tail streamed out behind it, a haze of shimmering stardust and fragments of rock.

48

Then BANG! The whole ship rocked and Nat and Joe were thrown back.

"Did we hit something, K?" asked Joe in a panic. But there was no answer.

Instead a message appeared on one of the screens.

I CAN'T SEE WHAT'S AHEAD. SOMETHING IN THE VIEWER MUST BE BROKEN. WE'LL HAVE TO STOP UNTIL WE FIND OUT WHAT IT IS AND FIX IT. I'LL TEST COMPUTER COMPONENTS. YOU CHECK THE REST.

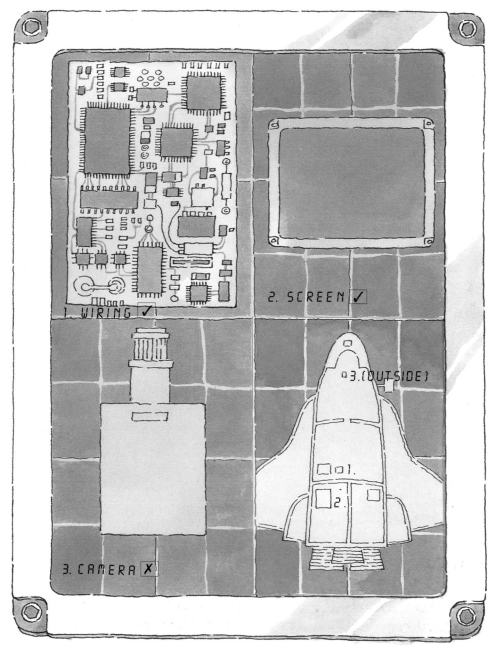

1. WIRING ✓

2. SCREEN ✓

3. (OUTSIDE)

1.

2.

3. CAMERA ✗

Where do we start?

Nat and Joe began to look around, but they didn't really know what they were looking for.

The engines stopped and the ship grew quiet. Soon the only sound was a faint hum from K.

Nat looked at the control panel. One of the screens was covered with fuzzy lines. A moment later four pictures came up on another screen.

It was very clear which part was broken. They could even see where on the ship they would find it.

What needs mending?

Stepping outside

Nat and Joe quickly put on their suits. "How do we move outside?" said Joe.

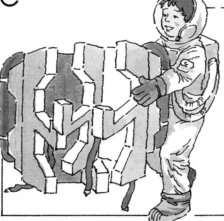

"Jet packs!" Nat told him pointing to a locker. Joe carried them over.

"These are like armchairs!" he said, leading the way outside.

The outer door opened, leaving Nat and Joe gazing out onto a million miles of blackness. For a second, it felt like they were the only two people in the universe.

Then Joe switched his jet pack on. "This is fun!" he yelled going one way.

"Better than football!" he shouted, going the other way.

"Try looping the loop!" he called to Nat from upside down.

Eventually they remembered why they had gone outside and started to look for the camera.

"It's down there," Joe said, pointing to the roof of the shuttle. "But it doesn't look broken to me."

They flew closer to investigate.

"The lens is broken and there's a hole in the panel on this side," Nat said as she put the tool box down.

Joe tried to unscrew the panel. But pushing on the screwdriver pushed him away from the ship.

Nat had to hold him in place, keeping herself still by holding a handle on the side of the ship.

As Joe took the panel off, he accidentally dropped one of the screws. It hung in space before him. "Amazing!" he said.

Nat sorted through all the new parts in the tool box. "I hope everything's here," she said. **Can you find what they need?**

51

Off to Mars

With the camera mended they flew on. The ship sped through space, but the journey to Mars still took a couple of hours.

As they neared the planet, one of the screens began to flash.

SOMETHING HAS GONE WRONG WITH THE AUTO PILOT. YOU'LL HAVE TO LAND THE SHIP. SWITCHING TO MANUAL NOW!

It was an urgent message from K. Joe watched in horror as Nat took control.

She grabbed the joystick, shut her eyes and pushed. The ship bumped to a halt.

Joe looked out in relief. "Hey, the sky's red! I bet it's hot out there," he said.

IT'S COMING FROM A DRY CHANNEL NOT FAR FROM THE SHIP, BETWEEN THREE POINTED ROCKS, A SQUARE ROCK AND A CRATER.

"No, you galaxy gazer, it's cold," said K as they put on their suits. "But there is a warm spot. How odd."

Nat and Joe hovered in the doorway as K told them what to look for, to find the warm spot.

Leaving the ship, Nat paused. "We'll be the first humans to walk on Mars. Anything could happen!"

They felt much heavier than they had on the moon. A wind blew dusty red sand all around them. Keeping together, they tried to look for the landmarks K had listed.

"Mars is covered in craters and rocks," Joe sighed. "We'll be here forever." But Nat thought she'd found the right place.

Can you see where they should go?

53

Into the planet

The light was so bright it hurt even through their tinted helmets.

Aliens from come you have where? Mars to welcome!

As their eyes grew used to the light, they looked around. They were surrounded by live rocks! Then the voice spoke again. It was talking backwards.

Did it call us aliens? We're not aliens!

Ssh! Er, hello! We come from Earth.

Front to back speak they where planet green blue the yes ah!

To their amazement Joe and Nat realized it was a rock they could hear in their heads! It spoke again and they saw pictures of its thoughts too.

All at talk didn't and hard and cold were they but flew they. Before Earth from visitors had we've.

Brains alien's the you are? Out came you when surprised were we. Them inside you like anything have didn't they.

Um, not exactly.

Landing bumpy very a had you. watch to stayed we so arrived you when surface the on up were we.

"We didn't see anyone when we landed," said Joe. "Where were you?"

Look back at page 53. How many rock people can you see?

The Martian caves

"Wow!" said Joe. "This is incredible. I can hardly believe it. Talking rocks!"

The voice in his head grew cross. "Rocks eat we. Martians we're rocks not we're. ROCKS?! Rocks?"

"Sorry," mumbled Joe.

A different voice entered their minds. "Way this! Mars of tour a like you'd perhaps?"

> There really is life on Mars!

> Cave rest the is this.

Nat and Joe followed the Martian down stone steps and into a large cave. It was full of sleeping, grunting rocks. They tiptoed through.

> Some like you would? Delicious! . . . umm.

> Er, no thank you.

> I ate earlier.

In the next cave, Martians were chipping rocks from the walls. Their guide picked up a chunk to chew.

"They must have iron teeth!" Joe whispered.

They climbed down to the third cave. One Martian was weaving cloth on a large stone frame. Another was leaning over a stone sink mixing paint and splashing it everywhere.

In the fourth cave they arrived in the middle of a concert.

Suddenly the music stopped. Their guide looked surprised.

"Visitor another?!" he said. "Alien flying another seen has scouts our of one."

To Nat and Joe's alarm, a picture of a spaceship appeared in their minds.

Why are they worried?

A new arrival

I always wanted to be an astronaut. Finally I flew to the moon.

I was stuck on board at first. But later, I stayed on the moon as part of an experiment.

Then disaster! Before I could fly back to Earth, my ship exploded.

I was stranded. For a while I didn't mind. I was sure someone would rescue me in the end. But no one came.

So I built a base using things other astronauts had left behind. Then I built robots for company. I even built two rockets. But I didn't know if they would fly, so I launched the first one empty.

Finally I made a satellite dish to beam messages to other life forms. But nobody replied. I'm a scientist and explorer. I need new challenges. I need new places to explore.

Mars explore could you.

As he finished, five Martians appeared. The astronaut looked shocked. "Have I gone crazy? I can hear voices in my head!" he said.

You do?

It to happened what know don't we but moon the from off take made you rocket first the saw we. Us it's crazy not you're!

Heading for home

"The ship I made reached Earth?" said the astronaut when Nat told him. He could hardly believe it. "What's so funny?" he asked, as Martians began to stream out from under the ground, all rolling around with laughter.

A Martian grinned. "One were you thought planet your on people the and aliens see to wanted you!"

The astronaut smiled too. "Keep your ship!" he said to Nat and Joe. "I can't wait to explore Mars."

"You'd better hurry home before someone notices you've gone and a brand new spaceship is missing."

Within minutes they were back on board and out of their spacesuits.

"You won't believe it, K," cried Nat. "We found aliens on Mars!"

"I think you've been in space too long," K said.

Down to Earth

"You poor things, stuck in a model for twenty minutes."

"Seat belts on, you alien spotters!" K said firmly as the engines roared to zoom them back to Earth.

"Nearly home!" K added as Earth appeared on the screen, growing bigger and bigger . . .

The next thing they knew the ship's door opened and a man was helping them out.

Feeling puzzled they went in search of their class. "It's as if we never took off," said Joe, putting his hands in his pockets. They felt very full.

Curiously he emptied everything onto a table. There it was, proof they really had been to space.

Which things did they bring back from space? Look back through the book to see where they found them.

Facts about space

Nat and Joe spent the rest of the day in the Space Experience. They found out lots of facts about the places they had visited. Later they made a display for their classroom wall.

There is no weather on the moon, so the footprints left by astronauts will be there for ten million years.

The moon takes the same time to turn around as it does to go around the Earth. This means that one side is always facing away from the Earth.

The first men landed on the moon in 1969 and the last ones in 1972. They left over 50000kg (110230lb) of litter.

Comets are made of ice and dust. Some scientists call them dirty snowballs. As a comet comes close to the sun, the sun's heat melts some of the ice. This forms the comet's tail.

Asteroids are rocks which circle the sun between Mars and Jupiter. Some are small but the biggest is about the size of France.

The moon only has one-sixth of Earth's gravity. Everything feels a sixth as heavy on the moon as it does on Earth.

The rings around Saturn and Uranus are made of millions of chunks of ice and can be seen from Earth.

Only three space craft have ever been as far out in the solar system as Saturn. The last one, Voyager 2, took four years to reach Saturn. It went on to visit Uranus and Neptune.

by Nat and Joe

Answers to puzzles

pages 36-37 Into space

The helmets are in a locker behind Nat. It is circled in this picture.

pages 38-39 Walking on the moon

Nat has noticed these extra footprints. Some of them cover the astronauts' footprints so they are newer, but they are different from Nat and Joe's.

pages 40-41
Men on the moon?

Joe saw the man before on this poster in the Space Experience.

pages 42-43 Escape

Joe can make the robots go back to their base by pressing the combination 317*. Nat remembers seeing it on a piece of paper on the astronaut's desk in the base.

pages 44-45
Computer speak

The way through the asteroids is shown in black.

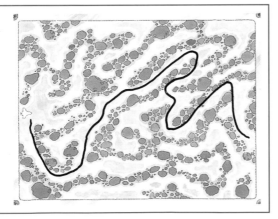

pages 46-47
A gas giant

The only planet Joe and Nat can land on is Mars. The gas planets have no solid surface and all the others apart from Earth are too far away or too close to the sun.

pages 48-49
Comet clash

The camera is the part which is broken. The fourth picture shows that it is outside the ship.

pages 50-51
Stepping outside

The parts they need are circled below.

pages 52-53
Off to Mars

The landmarks are circled below. The warm spot is marked with an X.

pages 54-55
Into the planet

There are nine rock people on page 53. They are circled in this picture.

pages 56-57
The Martian caves

Nat and Joe are worried that the astronaut from the moon is landing on Mars. They saw this picture of the rocket in his base on the moon.

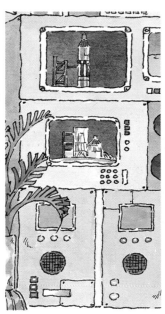

pages 58-59
A new arrival

The ship reached Earth. There was a picture of it on display at the Space Experience on page 34. It is under the label "Alien ship?"

Alien ship?

Ryan Rocket

Landed on Earth 1995

page 61   Down to Earth

These are the things Joe brought back from space.

A piece of rock from Mars.

A broken lens from the ship's camera.

A piece of rock from the moon.

The remote control from the base on the moon.

A straw from the drink with his meal.

Wire and a screw from the ship's camera.

A scrap of cloth made by the Martians.

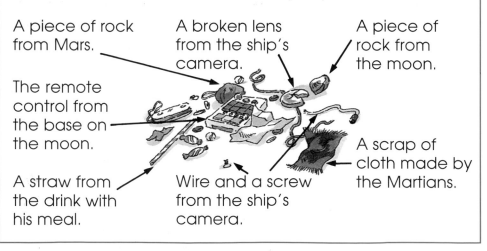

PUZZLE JOURNEY
THROUGH TIME

Who would have thought that an amazing adventure could
start with the toss of an old coin? But that's exactly what happens
to Matt and Lou when they stay with their Aunt Hattie, one summer.
Join Matt and Lou as they whirl through time, and see if you can
solve the puzzles they face. The answers are at the end
of the story if you are stuck.

Matt   Lou

Prior Place
Giddyham
July 16th

Dear Matt and Lou,

I'm so pleased you're spending the summer holidays with me. I'm sure you'll have fun exploring my rambling old house – it's full of history. We can go for cycle rides and picnics too. I'll pick you up from the station on Thursday. See you soon!

love Aunt Hattie xx

See you later, dears.

Where shall we look first?

Auntie thought it might be in the attic.

Matt and Lou had been staying with Aunt Hattie for a week, when she had to go out. She had been in the middle of searching for her photograph album. "Let's find the album for her as a surprise," Lou said to Matt.

In the attic

The attic was huge, and full of junk. They stared at the chaos in dismay. The album could be anywhere. Matt stumbled as he stepped off the ladder.

"Oh no," he groaned. "There goes a marble. Now we'll have to find that, too."

Matt spied his marble under a table. It was next to an unusual little box.

Matt picked up the box and rattled it at Lou. "It's quite heavy," he said.

It was full of odd things. Matt put in his marble, and picked out a coin.

"Heads or tails?" he asked, as he flipped the coin.

The coin shone brightly as it flew into the air. Lou watched it spinning in the dusty sunlight.

She had a funny feeling in her stomach, as if she were whizzing around on a merry-go-round. Matt looked rather pale, too.

67

The Viking village

The feeling passed as Matt caught the coin. But now they were surrounded by noise, as if someone had turned on a radio. Peculiar smells wafted past. Even their clothes were different. But Matt still had the box from Aunt Hattie's attic.

Where did these clothes come from?

What's happened? This isn't the attic.

"Where are we?" asked Matt. Lou peeped out from under the table and blinked in disbelief.

The room was full of people wearing funny clothes. They were eating, drinking and singing.

As Lou stood up, a bone bounced off her head. She heard voices behind her, and turned in surprise.

Go and get Harald, you two. He's going to miss Leif's speech.

You know his house. He's got hens everywhere.

They need proper directions. Go down to the sea and turn left by the ship. Turn right toward the pond, then right again by the sheep pen. That'll get you there.

Lou dragged Matt outside.
"Look at that ship," he said,
clutching the box. "It's like the
Viking one we made at school."

"Vikings!" said Lou. "I think we
should find Harald, whoever
he is, and ask him some
questions."

**Can you see which house
is Harald's?**

In Harald's house

In a few minutes, they were outside Harald's house. The door opened as Matt knocked on it.

As their eyes adjusted to the gloom, they could see a large figure hunched over the fire.

He stood up and towered over the children. Lou hurriedly babbled some questions.

Harald stared at them, baffled and amused. "Am I a Viking? What sort of question is that?" he chuckled.

"And I know Leif Ericsson has been away for years, but you must have heard of him." He launched into a long story.

Leif is a relative of mine.

He lives in Greenland, so we haven't seen him for years.

He's quite an explorer. A few years back, he discovered a new land, west of Greenland.

He found vines growing there. So he called it Vinland.

But the locals are quite fierce, so no one has settled there for long.

He's going to tell us about his travels after the feast. I must go back.

He left the house, muttering, "Am I a Viking? Silliest thing I ever heard..."

Matt sat down on a bench. "I think they really are Vikings," he said.

He picked up Harald's carving, and accidentally knocked Aunt Hattie's box off the bench. Its contents scattered over the floor.

They started putting things back in the box. Matt saw some paper wedged in the bottom. "It looks like a letter," he said. It tore as he pulled it out.

Lou laid the pieces on the floor. They could still read the letter. It seemed to be written to their Aunt Hattie.

"It's about time travel," she gasped, picking up a last coin. "Is that what we've done?"

"Let's try it and see," said Matt. He took a carved green stone from the box.

Can you read the letter?

"Hattie, my dearest child,
This box and the things in it will help you travel through time. Throw and catch any object in h... ...ere, and it will take you to the time ...and place that it came from.

You will under...stand and be able to speak every langu...age you may hear. Y... will also chan...ge to fit in ...clothes

Be ...careful not to ...lose this box ...it, you could be trapped in another ...sun ...without time forever

Your loving Father."

71

A fireworks party

Matt threw the stone. They felt dizzy. Then it went dark. It worked!

The air was warm and scented now. Voices were approaching, and a light.

They shrank behind a bush to listen. What were the voices discussing?

Slowly, the speakers came closer. Now Matt could see they were two women, carrying a lantern.

Lou was intrigued by the conversation. "Let's follow them. We might find out more," she whispered.

They fell into step behind the women. "All right," hissed Matt. "But where are we - and when?"

The path led through an exotic garden. In the distance, they could see an impressive building.

"It looks like the Chinese palace in Aunt Hattie's album," said Matt. "But what is this monster?"

A crowd gathered in front of the building. They hushed as a giraffe was led past. A voice announced, "This fabulous animal has been sent to our Emperor from Africa."

Lou was astonished. "It's not a monster at all! They can't have seen a giraffe before. How long ago is this?"

"I don't know," said Matt. "But there aren't any cars or electric lights."

"That's odd, I'm sure I saw a..." said Lou. Her words were drowned out by the bang of fireworks exploding.

Matt watched the display. He remembered that fireworks were an old Chinese invention. But Lou was puzzled. She fingered the coin she had picked up in Harald's house.

Lou saw something that didn't belong. Can you see what it was?

When in Rome

Lou dropped the coin and caught it. At once, she and Matt were in a busy street.

A hand gripped Matt by the shoulder. He tried to pull away, but it held on harder.

"Take these dormice to the kitchen," the man said. "You young slaves should be working."

He hurried them along the street. The scene around them looked like a picture of Ancient Rome, even down to the people in tunics and sandals. "So now we're Roman slaves," exclaimed Lou.

Soon they arrived at a palace. Matt and Lou were sent to the kitchen and set to work. They listened to the other slaves gossiping, and found out that they were preparing dinner for the Emperor Caligula and eight guests.

Flavia looks silly in her blonde wigs, but Petronius can't leave her alone.

Well, Julius is old enough to be Cornelia's father.

I love that brooch Livia wears. It's always on her left shoulder.

Incitatus* is coming. He'll be late, as usual.

That's the sauce ready for the dormice.

Marcus is a mess. His clothes are awful, and his sandals are falling apart.

Servius is back from Syria. He'll be so suntanned!

A few hours later, they went to take the guests' cloaks as they arrived. Matt remembered the gossip from the kitchen. He could tell who was who.

But soon he was worried. "That one's an impostor," he hissed. "She doesn't fit any of the descriptions."

Who is he talking about?

*say "In-sit-ah-tus".

75

Dinner with the Emperor

Lou and Matt were told to serve at the banquet. It was a strange affair. All the guests lay down around the table, and they picked up the food and ate with their fingers.

"We'd never get away with manners like that at home," muttered Matt.

Incitatus, my dear! So glad you could make it!

The guests were happily eating dormice and other weird dishes when a man brought in a horse. The Emperor rushed over, and greeted the horse.

"Incitatus is a horse!" giggled Lou. "Is this a joke?" But none of the diners even looked up.

The other guests greeted Incitatus, as he wandered around the room. Matt and Lou dashed around, passing plates and pouring wine.

Meanwhile, the Emperor settled down to chat with the guest they thought was an impostor. As Lou was topping up their wine, she heard something that made her blood run cold.

"Have him murdered. It's sure to work."

Lou was so shocked, she didn't hear the horse come up behind her.

It nudged into her. Not thinking, she sharply pushed its head away.

Then she dropped the jug. Wine spilled all over the Emperor's feet.

"Matt! Help!"

"Guards!" he shrieked. "Take this slave away and kill her! She has dropped wine on me and insulted Senator Incitatus!"

Lou yelled, "Get the box! We must move on!" But Matt had put the box in a safe place, and he couldn't remember where.

Can you see the box?

77

Early days

Matt hurriedly threw Lou a flint from the box. At once, they escaped through time.

Now they were in a quiet, snowy landscape. As soon as Lou saw their clothes, she started to laugh.

Their Roman tunics had been replaced by smelly skins, sewn together with leather thongs.

A woman appeared from a cave behind them. She asked them to come in.

Inside, people were sitting around a fire, eating. An old man was telling stories.

After a few minutes, Matt noticed some men taking lamps and going out into the snow. "Where are they going?" he murmured, curiously.

He and Lou followed them silently out of the cave, and through the snowy woods.

The men disappeared into an opening in the hillside. The children followed them into a cave with fantastic paintings of animals on the walls. The men stood on tree trunks to work on the pictures.

But then one of the men noticed them. "You know you shouldn't be here," he said. "These paintings are sacred to our clan. Go now and I won't tell anyone."

The snow's filled up our tracks.

Lou and Matt slunk out into the snow. They tried to remember the way back to the other cave.

They soon realized they were lost. But then they saw some tracks that looked like a dog's.

"The dog must belong to the cave men," said Lou. "If we follow the tracks, they'll lead us back."

What's that?

The tracks led them deep into the forest. From time to time, a wailing noise broke the silence.

Now they realized what had left the tracks. They were surrounded by a pack of wolves.

There seemed to be no way to escape.

What should they do now?

Knights on horseback

Matt's hand shook as he threw a golden brooch. Just in time...

Lou looked around. "The Middle Ages," she said. "I hope we'll be safe here."

They were surrounded by merry people, laughing and joking.

The main attraction was jousting. It drew the children like a magnet.

It was exciting and scary to watch the knights charging at each other.

Lou and Matt squeezed through the crowd to get a better view.

All of a sudden, a woman appeared out of thin air, right between the knights who were jousting.

Matt dashed forward, and tripped. He dropped the box, but ran on, too excited to notice.

As Lou ran after Matt, she heard two women. She didn't realize they were talking about the box.

The mysterious person vanished as suddenly as she had appeared. The fallen knight groaned.

He looked up, bleary-eyed, then lay down again. "What on earth is that?" he asked.

Matt saw that several things had changed.

Can you see what they are?

Around the castle

"I don't like this," gabbled Matt. "There are modern things appearing. I think that person brought them. Let's get out of here."

It was then he realized he had lost the box. They had to find it, or they would be here forever!

Now Lou understood. It must have been their box that the woman Meg picked up. She was taking it to the castle. They had to get it back, and fast.

We have to find this Meg and follow her.

When she goes into a room, we'll drop behind her.

If she leaves the box, we'll slip in and get it.

As she spoke, a cart full of people drove past. Meg was on board! Quickly, they jumped onto the cart behind it.

Now they were on their way to the castle, and the box was only just out of reach.

Once they were inside the castle wall, Lou began to worry. This wasn't going to be easy. The castle was enormous, and there were people everywhere. Worse still, most of the women were dressed like Meg.

"Look very carefully, Matt," said Lou. "We mustn't lose her."

Can you see which person is Meg?

All at sea

At last they had the box back. Lou threw an earring and they arrived in a wooden room. Outside, they could hear splashing noises. The air smelled fishy, and the floor was moving. "We're on a ship," said Matt.

To Captain Abel Tasman,

Good luck on your voyage of discovery. I hope you will find the new southern continent, and open up new trade routes. Don't forget to name the land after me.

You have probably heard tales of a pirate who appears on ships as if by magic. She steals the most valuable things and leaves strange objects that no one has ever seen. Don't let these silly stories put you off.

From Governor-General Van Diemen of the Dutch East India Company.

Matt caught a piece of paper as it fell off a desk. It was covered in scrawly foreign writing. But as he stared at it, it seemed to turn into English.

Lou read it over his shoulder. "This pirate business - it sounds like what happened at the joust."

Matt's eyes lit up. "Do you suppose it could be the same woman?"

Before they could discuss it, the door swung open and the captain stalked in.

They couldn't think how to explain, as he hauled them out of the cabin.

He shook Matt roughly. "So are you stowaways? Or spies for the pirates?"

Up on the ship's deck, the captain got a sailor to tie their hands.

They listened while the ship's crew debated what to do with them.

Soon, with land in sight, the captain made his decision.

A sailor rowed Matt and Lou ashore and helped them out of the boat, as kindly as he dared.

As he left, the sailor saw something on the beach. He wrapped it up and put it in the box.

Then he rowed away.

How can Matt and Lou free themselves?

On the wagon

Lou cut the ropes with the knife. Matt threw a bullet in the air. Instantly, they were in a covered cart, full of household junk.

Outside, a line of wagons stretched as far as Matt could see. Women were walking alongside, and farther off, men on horseback were driving cattle across the plain. "The Wild West," breathed Matt.

"Hi, I'm Jesse Applegate," said a boy, running up. He thrust a hand at Matt and pulled him down.

"How are you folks?" he added. "Do you want to play?"

Lou jumped down, and joined in the rowdy game they were playing around the wagons. She would wait to show Matt what she had found in the wagon.

Stop, thief!

Suddenly, there was a shriek from one of the wagons.

A woman was crying. "Someone has stolen my necklace. It was the only valuable thing we had."

At last Lou could show Matt the poster she had found. "Matt, look!" she whispered. "Do you recognize her? It's the impostor from the Roman banquet. She's been here."

Matt recognized her as the woman at the joust, too, and remembered the letter on the ship. "Perhaps she really will change history," he said. "We have to stop her."

He looked more closely at the poster. "Well, we know where to follow her to," he said, putting his hand in the box.

Where are they going to go?

WANTED

Fools! Do you think you can stop me? Soon I shall be the richest woman in the universe! Next stop: Then I'll change history as I choose!

FOR BANK ROBBERY AND JAIL BREAKING

The notorious bank robber, Anna Krannism, has disappeared from her jail cell. She may be heading West on the Oregon Trail. If you see her, arrest her, and hand her over to the authorities.

REWARD

87

The Pharaoh's trail

Lou caught the beetle-shaped Egyptian charm. The dusty American desert vanished.

Now they were in a rocky landscape, eerily lit by the moon. They flattened themselves against a rock and listened to a voice giving orders.

> Obey me. I am more powerful than your Pharaoh.

> Lead me to the tomb. When we're in, reseal it and leave me to it.

> But the tomb of King Tutankhamun...

> What if we are cursed for this? The valley is sacred.

> Move it, worms! Your punishment will be greatest if you fail me.

"That must be Anna Krannism. What's she up to here?" said Matt.

"She's bullying them into robbing a tomb," gasped Lou. "That's horrid."

Soon the villains were moving off. "We'll follow them," said Matt.

> It must be the Valley of the Kings.

Lou and Matt trailed the threesome along a path. It went steeply down into a dry, rocky valley.

Lou tripped over a rock. A hail of sand and loose stones tumbled down in front of her.

As the villains looked around, the children ducked down behind a rock - just in time to hide.

When they came out, Anna Krannism and her men had gone. They followed the path to the bottom of the valley and found a maze of paths leading in every direction.

Lou took the "Wanted" poster out of the box again. She hoped it might hold another clue.

Moonlight caught the back of the poster. There was a map scribbled on it.

Lou smoothed out the poster, and they stared at it, turning it to match the scene that lay before them.

X the treasure awaits me here

shows a known tomb!

"That's funny," said Matt. "The X doesn't seem to show an actual tomb." In a flash, he realized that the X marked something beside a tomb. Now he knew where to go.

Where is Anna Krannism hiding?

Tutankhamun's tomb

A bang and a blinding flash came from behind the pile of rubble. They must be on the right track.

"After you," said Lou, looking doubtfully at the passage that was blasted down into the ground.

Then she heard footsteps behind her. But before she could warn Matt, something hit her head.

When Lou came to, her hands were tied, and she was in a small room full of golden treasure.

Matt was slumped beside her. Anna Krannism snarled at them, "You can't stop me now, fools!"

"I have the best treasures of history," she crowed. "And I've replaced them with modern things!"

She laughed loudly at their bewildered faces. "But I must leave you," she continued. "Howard Carter will open the tomb in 3000 years. I'm sure he'll find you very intriguing!"

"Howard who?" muttered Matt.

Anna Krannism laughed again. She grabbed hold of a golden statue. Then she threw a silver card in the air.

Instantly, she and the statue vanished. Now Matt and Lou were alone in the Pharaoh's tomb.

Lou wriggled behind Matt. She tugged desperately at the rope around his wrists. It came loose!

Matt untied Lou. Then he grabbed the box, saying "We've got something that will help us chase her."

He had seen it in the box when they first found it.

Can you see it on page 67?

Into the future

In a flash, they were in a strange room full of books and treasures from all sorts of times and places. They spotted a huge chest in one corner, marked "Time Travel Kit."

Anna Krannism appeared at the other side of the room. She was brandishing a nasty-looking weapon.

> You meddling kids again! You'll never keep me from ruling the world!

Time Travel Kit

> The Time Police!

Suddenly, Anna Krannism was trapped in a laser cage. Three men in silver suits rushed in, ready to arrest her.

> I'm Inspector Marconi.

Two of the men led Anna Krannism away. The third introduced himself to Matt and Lou. "I need your help," he said.

> She usually leaves something in each place.

> There were the things at the joust...

"I have to collect all the modern things Anna's left in history," he explained. "Did you notice anything that didn't belong?"

Back home

They told Marconi all they had seen. Then Lou threw the marble Matt had put in the box when he first found it.

In an instant, they were back in the attic, and in their own clothes. Matt looked at his watch. No time had passed.

"Lou," he said, "Did anything really happen?" As he spoke, the sailor's gift fell out of the box, still wrapped in its rag.

Matt unwrapped the gift. It was an egg, and a crack was spreading across it. He set it on the floor.

After a moment's suspense, an odd little bird struggled out of the shell. Lou laughed, "Inspector Marconi has gone to find the things that don't belong in history. Let's hope he doesn't find our little dodo - they're supposed to be extinct."

Look back through the book. Can you find all the things Anna Krannism left behind?

Aunt Hattie's history notes

When Lou and Matt found the photo album, a bundle of papers tied with a blue ribbon fell out. They were all notes on history. Some were about the places Matt and Lou had been to. They spread the papers on the floor to read them.

Upper~class Roman dinners often included bizarre dishes, like stuffed dormice, just for the sake of novelty.

The Chinese invented gunpowder, and used it for fireworks long before they made war with it. In the 1400s, they made voyages to Africa. A giraffe was sent to the Emperor as a curiosity.

King Edward III of England and his successors held famous tournaments. Many were held near Windsor Castle. Windsor is still a home of the British royal family.

The most famous wagon train to travel the Oregon Trail was called the Great Emigration, as there were over 1000 settlers. One of the people who later wrote memoirs was Jesse Applegate, who was seven when he made the journey.

1922 - The find of the century
The tomb of Tutankhamun was "lost" when another tomb was built above it. It was rediscovered by Howard Carter and Lord Carnarvon. It was broken into twice in ancient times, but very little was taken. No other tomb has been found to rival it.

A Roman historian says that the Emperor Caligula's horse, Incitatus, worked as a senator in his government. The horse was often invited to banquets, and held dinner parties himself, in his marble stable in the palace.

About 17,000 years ago, Cro-Magnon men created magnificent animal paintings in caves in central France. Some of the most spectacular paintings are at Lascaux. They were found in 1940 by 4 young men.

One of the great Norse sagas (stories of the Vikings), says that Leif Ericsson was a son of Erik the Red of Greenland. He sailed to North America (which he called Vinland), about 1000 AD. He arrived there about 400 years before Christopher Columbus.

Before Australia was discovered, people thought there must be a continent there. The Dutch East India Company sent Abel Tasman to look for it in 1642. He claimed a small island to the south of Australia, which he named Van Diemen's Land (now called Tasmania). Then he sailed around the mainland without ever seeing it. On the way, he stopped at Mauritius, the island where dodos lived.

Answers to puzzles

pages 68-69   **The Viking village**

Harald's house is circled in red. The route Matt and Lou must take to get there is shown in red.

pages 70-71   **In Harald's house**
The note says:

Hattie, my dearest child,
   This box and the things in it will help you travel through time. Throw and catch any object in here, and it will take you to the time and place that it came from.
   You will understand and be able to speak every language you may hear. Your clothes will also change to fit in.
   Be careful not to lose this box - without it, you could be trapped in another time forever.   Your loving Father.

pages 72-73   **A fireworks party**

Lou saw this boy using a flashlight. But Matt noticed there were no electric lights.

pages 74-75   **When in Rome**

This is the impostor. She is pretending to be Livia, but she is wearing her brooch on her right shoulder, not her left.

All the other guests match the slaves' descriptions. The guest who is missing is Incitatus – the slaves said he would be late.

pages 76-77   **Dinner with the Emperor**

The box is under the couch on the left of the picture of the big banqueting scene. It is circled in red.

pages 78-79   **Early days**

The only way Lou and Matt can escape from the wolves is to throw something from the box and go to another time.

pages 80-81   **Knights on horseback**

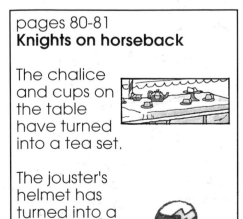

The chalice and cups on the table have turned into a tea set.

The jouster's helmet has turned into a motorcycle helmet.

pages 82-83   **Around the castle**

Meg is circled in red.

pages 84-85   **All at sea**

The sailor dropped his knife. They can use it to cut their ropes.

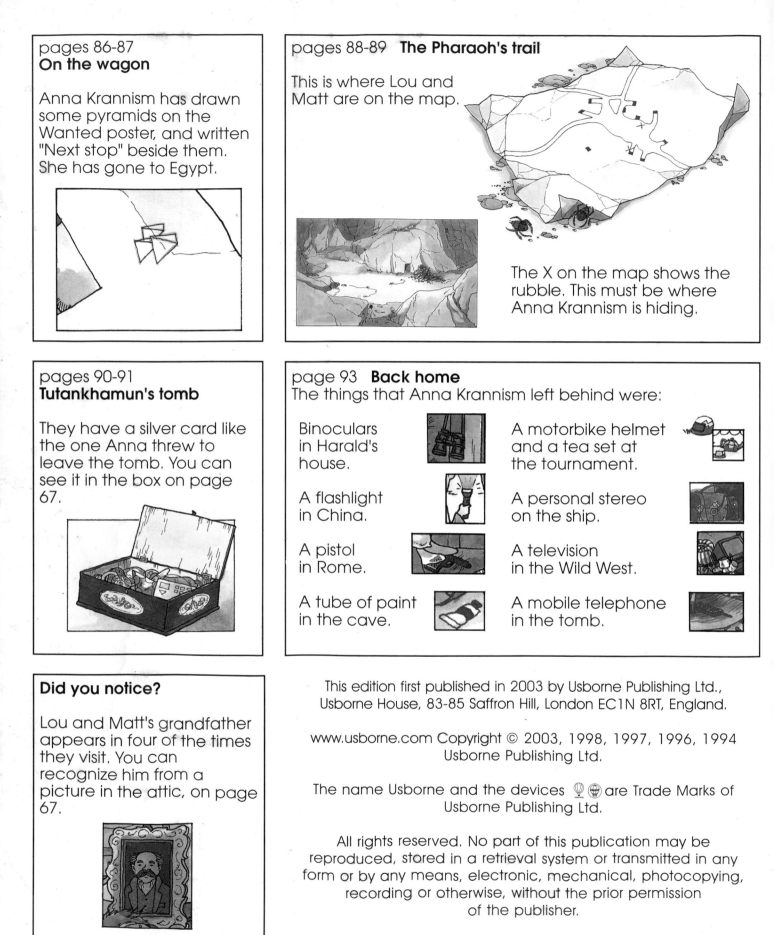

pages 86-87
On the wagon

Anna Krannism has drawn some pyramids on the Wanted poster, and written "Next stop" beside them. She has gone to Egypt.

pages 88-89 The Pharaoh's trail

This is where Lou and Matt are on the map.

The X on the map shows the rubble. This must be where Anna Krannism is hiding.

pages 90-91
Tutankhamun's tomb

They have a silver card like the one Anna threw to leave the tomb. You can see it in the box on page 67.

page 93 Back home
The things that Anna Krannism left behind were:

Binoculars in Harald's house.

A flashlight in China.

A pistol in Rome.

A tube of paint in the cave.

A motorbike helmet and a tea set at the tournament.

A personal stereo on the ship.

A television in the Wild West.

A mobile telephone in the tomb.

Did you notice?

Lou and Matt's grandfather appears in four of the times they visit. You can recognize him from a picture in the attic, on page 67.

This edition first published in 2003 by Usborne Publishing Ltd., Usborne House, 83-85 Saffron Hill, London EC1N 8RT, England.

www.usborne.com Copyright © 2003, 1998, 1997, 1996, 1994 Usborne Publishing Ltd.

The name Usborne and the devices 🎈 🐝 are Trade Marks of Usborne Publishing Ltd.

U.E. Printed in Portugal. First published in America 1999.